This Topsy and Tim book belongs to

_____

Topsy and Tim
Learn to Swim

By Jean and Gareth Adamson

Consultants: the asa

the asa
the essential element

Illustrations by Belinda Worsley

A catalogue record for this book is available from the British Library

Published by Ladybird Books Ltd
A Penguin Company
Penguin Books Ltd., 80 Strand, London WC2R 0RL, UK
Penguin Books Australia Ltd., 707 Collins Street, Melbourne, Victoria 3008, Australia
Penguin Group (NZ) 67 Apollo Drive, Rosedale, North Shore 0632, New Zealand

010

© Jean and Gareth Adamson MCMXCV
Reissued MMXIV

ISBN: 978-1-40930-060-1
Printed in China

www.topsyandtim.com

Topsy and Tim were learning to swim. Mummy took them to the swimming pool nearly every day.

Mummy helped them put on their swimming things and blow up their armbands. She put their clothes safely in a locker.

On the way to the pool there were showers,
to make sure they were nice and clean.

There was a small pool for beginners like Topsy
and Tim. It was full of happy, noisy children.
"Race you to the water!" shouted Topsy.
Topsy's feet skidded. Mr Pollack the swimming
instructor rushed to save her.

"Never run near the pool," he said. "The floor is wet and slippery and it's very hard if you fall and bang your head."

Topsy and Tim went down the steps into the pool.
Mummy went in with them. The water came up to
Topsy and Tim's middles.

They held on to the rail and kicked as hard as they could. Mummy did get splashed.
"Stretch your legs out," she said.

"Now let me see you swim dog-paddle," said Mummy. Topsy
paddled like a puppy. Her armbands helped her to float.

Tim paddled hard. He
splashed more than Topsy,
but his legs kept sinking.

"Do you think you could swim without your armbands?" asked Mummy.
"Of course," shouted Tim.
"I'm a champion swimmer."

First Topsy stood in the water a few steps from
the side. Then she pushed forward in the water
and dog-paddled to the hand rail.

"Well done, Topsy," said Mummy.

"You can really swim now."

Then it was Tim's turn. He tried hard... but his feet would not float.
"Never mind," said Mummy. "You must put your armbands back on."

"Can I help?" said a kind voice. It was Mr Pollack, the swimming instructor. He told Tim to bob right down until the water was up to his chin.
"Now walk along and pull the water back with your hands," he said.

Tim paddled hard with his hands, then he
kicked up and down with his legs.
"Look at me," he gasped. "I'm swimming!"
And he really was.

Mummy helped them to get dressed and dry their hair. "Won't Dad be surprised when we tell him we can swim without our armbands," said Tim.

Dad was waiting for them in the snack bar.
"Dad, we can swim!" cried Topsy.
Dad was pleased.

He pointed to a poster on the wall.
"There's going to be a swimming competition,"
he said. "You can swim in the beginners' race,
Topsy and Tim."

The next week Dad and Mummy and Topsy
and Tim went to the big pool for the swimming
competition.
There were short races.
There were long races.

There was a race for children swimming on their backs.
Last of all there was the beginners' race in the beginners' pool.

Mr Pollack blew his whistle to start the race.
Topsy swam dog-paddle as fast as she could.
Tim was left behind – but he knew what to do.

He bobbed right down in the water until it reached his chin, then he paddled hard with his hands and feet. Everyone cheered as the children swam slowly across the pool.

Topsy and Tim didn't win the race, but everyone got a Beginners' Badge because they had all reached the other side.

*Now turn the page and help
Topsy and Tim solve a puzzle.*

Can you help Topsy and Tim swim to Mummy at the other side of the pool? They must try not to bump into the other people.

A Map of the Village

farm

Topsy and
Tim's house

Tony's
house

Kerry
house

park